Carry Me, Mama

Story by Monica Devine
Paintings by Pauline Paquin

Fitzhenry & Whiteside

Text Copyright © 2001 by Monica Devine
Illustrations Copyright © 2001 by Pauline Paquin

First published by Fitzhenry & Whiteside in paperback in 2005.
Published by Stoddart Kids in 2001.

Published in Canada by
Fitzhenry & Whiteside,
195 Allstate Parkway,
Markham, Ontario
L3R 4T8

Published in the United States by
Fitzhenry & Whiteside,
121 Harvard Avenue, Suite 2,
Allston, Massachusetts
02134

www.fitzhenry.ca   godwit@fitzhenry.ca

10 9 8 7 6 5 4 3 2 1

Library and Archives Canada Cataloguing in Publication
Devine, Monica
Carry me, Mama / Monica Devine ; illustrations by Pauline Paquin.

ISBN 1-55005-150-4

1. Inuit—Juvenile fiction. I. Paquin, Pauline, 1952- II. Title.

PZ7.D48Ca 2005   J813'.54   C2005-900367-7

U.S. Publisher Cataloging-in-Publication Data
(Library of Congress Standards)
Devine, Monica
Carry me, Mama / story by Monica Devine ; illustrations by Pauline Paquin.

Originally published: Toronto : Stoddart Kids, 2001.

[32] p. : col. ill. ; cm.

Summary: Katie has viewed life from the safety of her mother's parka, one spring her mother decides that it is
time for Katie to walk on her own. Katie is overwhelmed and begs, "Carry me, Mama!" but Mama knows that
it is time for Katie to walk on her own.

ISBN 1-55005-150-4

1. Mother and child – Fiction – Juvenile literature. 2. Inuit children – Juvenile fiction. I. Paquin, Pauline, 1952- .
II. Title.

[E] 22   PZ7.E8564Ca 2005

*Fitzhenry & Whiteside acknowledges with thanks the Canada
Council for the Arts, the Government of Canada through the Book
Publishing Industry Development Program (BPIDP), and the
Ontario Arts Council for their support of our publishing program.*

Printed and bound in Hong Kong, China
by Book Art Inc., Toronto

In loving memory of Helena Marzonie.
When I was only three, we began our "walks".
— M. D.

To my sons, Jonathan, Marc, Antoine, and Jean-Olivier,
who have always been an endless source of inspiration,
and to my husband who has always believed in me.
— P. P.

When Katie was a baby, she went everywhere with Mama. She rode on Mama's back under her big, flowery parka.

When the river ran high and swift, Katie went with Mama to catch king salmon.

When the air chilled and the leaves turned to gold,
Katie went with Mama to the mountains.
Katie peered over Mama's shoulder as she stooped
to pick plump, red berries.

One spring day, Mama lifted Katie from her parka and said, "You're a big girl now, Katie. It's time for you to walk."

Katie did not want to walk. "Carry me, Mama," she said, but Mama paid her no mind. So Katie held Mama's hand and they walked — as far as you can throw a stone — to Aunt Nina's house.

Katie took big steps to keep up with Mama.

After a long while, Katie and Mama walked again —
as far as a rabbit runs — to Uncle Kalila's cabin.
Katie's boots sank deep in the mud and made squishy sounds
when she picked up her feet.

"Carry me, Mama," Katie said, but Mama paid her no mind.
So, Katie stepped in Mama's footprints. One, two, three
steps . . . four . . . Water rushed in and washed Mama's
footprints away.

Still, Katie kept walking.

Many moons later, Katie and Mama walked again — as far as a bear roams — to the village store. They walked across the frozen river, past the church, and up a steep hill.

Katie huffed and puffed. "Carry me, Mama," she said, but Mama paid her no mind. Katie's boots squeaked in the snow. Her knees quivered and her legs itched.

Still, Katie kept right on walking.

At the store, Mama bought rice and pickles and crackers.
Outside dark, heavy clouds raced across the sky.
On the way home, Katie hurried next to Mama.
Blowing snow whipped and whirled all around her.
The icy wind howled in her ears.

Mama stooped down and held Katie close.

"Carry me, Mama," Katie said.

"Look, Katie. Over there, where the ravens fly," said Mama.
"Soon we will be home."

So, Katie walked and walked, on and on. Down the steep hill she went. Across the frozen river she trudged. Past the church she shuffled, though her steps got smaller and smaller.

"Carry me, Mama," Katie said. Then she stopped. And looked up.

Ravens soared high above her.

Katie picked up her feet and swung her arms. The ravens
dove and swooped in front of her. She marched ahead
of Mama — faster and faster. Suddenly Katie ran.
Far off and away, Katie ran and ran and ran.

"We're home, Mama!"

Katie threw open the door and they both plopped down in Mama's big chair.

"Mama," Katie sighed. "When the river breaks up, can we walk to Grandpa's fish camp?"

"Oh, that's a very long way," said Mama.

"But I can walk far now, Mama," said Katie.
"As far as a rabbit runs, as far as a bear roams . . . as far as a raven flies, Mama. And all the way back home."
Katie yawned.

"Time for bed, now, Katie," said Mama.

"Carry me, Mama," Katie said, and Mama turned.
In an owl's blink she reached down, scooped Katie up in
her arms, and . . . *carried her!*

All the way to bed.